Hazel Mitchell

Mom had to go into the hospital, so Dad was taking me to Grandpa and Grandma's house for summer vacation.

Rabbit was coming, too. He likes car trips.

I looked out the window. Dad and I sang.

We ate snacks.

I thought about Mom.

Grandpa and Grandma were waiting for us.

After we ate dinner, Dad left.

Later, Grandma tucked me into bed.

The next day, I helped Grandma with the chores.

I drew a picture to send to Mom.

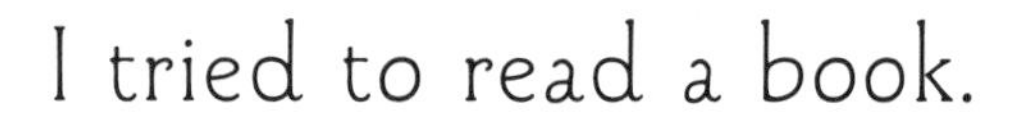

I tried to read a book.

But I couldn't concentrate.

Grandpa suggested I help him in the garden.

Grandpa's garden was full of flowers and vegetables. There were carrots and lettuce and daisies.

Grandpa showed me his prized sweet peas. He asked if I'd like to look after them. And I said yes.

Grandpa said I could enter the sweet peas in the flower show.

When I talked to Dad at bedtime, I told him about the sweet peas. He told me how Mom was doing.

The sweet peas were all different colors. Grandpa said the blue ones were the best, but they were the hardest to grow.

I did all the things that Grandpa showed me. I tied the stems to the canes. I removed old seedpods.

I pulled out the weeds.

I added Grandpa's secret formula to the water.

But one morning, something terrible happened. All the flower buds had fallen off the sweet peas.

Grandpa didn't know why, so I looked at his gardening books.

One book said the sweet peas might be too cold at night. I asked Grandpa for blankets and wrapped the plants up snugly.

But when I went to check the sweet peas in the morning, more buds had fallen.

I would have to try my next plan.

The summer days were very hot. I borrowed Grandma's umbrellas to shade the sweet peas.

But the shade from the umbrellas didn't help.

I only had one idea left.

Sweet peas need just the right amount of water around their roots. I watered them very carefully.

Suddenly icy cold water showered me and the sweet peas. And then I realized what was wrong! It was Grandpa.

He was watering his vegetables and drenching the sweet peas. The flower buds don't like icy cold water. That's why they were falling off.

"Grandpa, stop, stop!"

From then on, Grandpa kept the hose away from the sweet peas.

We checked for new flowers every day.

And, finally, we saw some new buds.

The next morning, I went into the garden. The sweet peas had flowered! And some of them were blue.

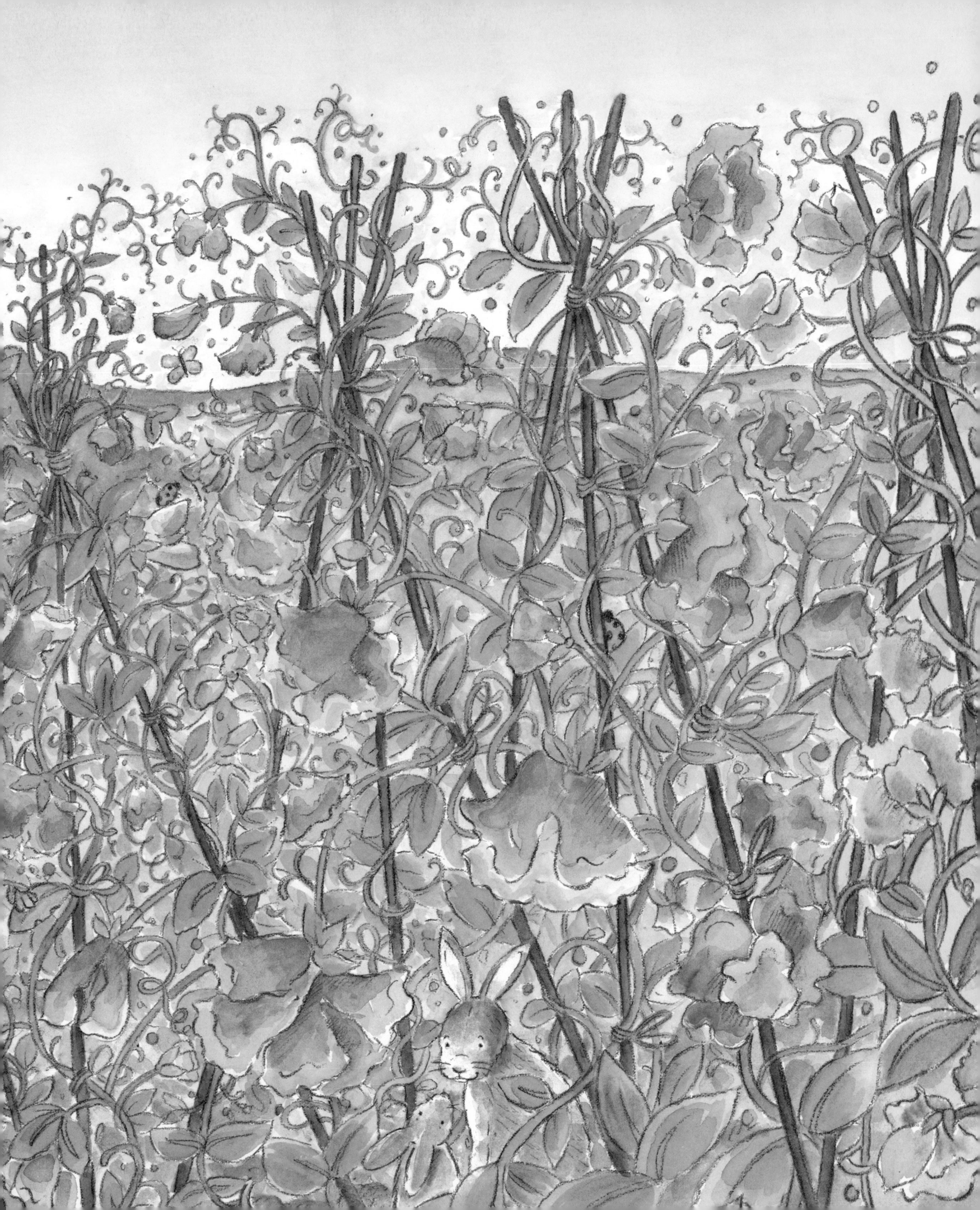

On the morning of the flower show,
Grandpa and I chose the best sweet peas.

Grandma helped me arrange the flowers in a special vase.

We walked to the flower show. Grandma carried her cake. Grandpa wheeled his vegetables, and I held my sweet peas.

All the sweet peas at the show looked much bigger and brighter than mine. But there were none as blue.

I put my sweet peas with the others for the judges, and we waited. When we went back to check, there was an envelope in front of my vase.

Inside was a certificate. My sweet peas had won a prize!

I should have felt happy, but I felt sad because Mom wasn't there. Then Grandma nudged me.

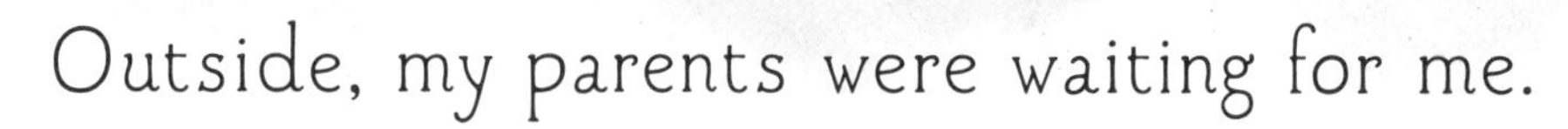
Outside, my parents were waiting for me.

I gave the sweet peas to Mom.

She was better, and we were going home.

Sweet Peas

Lathyrus odoratus

The sweet peas that we grow in our gardens today were introduced in England in 1699, when a Franciscan monk named Francisco Cupani sent a friend some of the seeds he had collected in Italy. There were five colors of sweet pea flowers at that time: black, maroon, scarlet, white, and pinkish red. Now there are hundreds of varieties to choose from.

In 1888, a Scottish gardener named Henry Eckford began a nursery for growing and cultivating sweet peas. He created many new types and colors of sweet peas, including a large variety called Grandiflora.

The first big competition, the British Sweet Pea Bi-Centenary Celebration, was held in London in 1900. Shortly thereafter, the British National Sweet Pea Society was formed.

Some of the new sweet peas are very easy to grow and are good to raise in both hot and cold climates. The sweet pea is an annual plant, which means that it completes its life cycle in a year and you must collect seedpods to regrow it the following year.

Now sweet peas are grown all over the world in all kinds of gardens for their color, fragrance, and beauty. And, of course, they are grown to show in competitions. One of the most popular colors is blue.

In memory of Elsie and Walter

 First edition 2021. Library of Congress Catalog Card Number pending. ISBN 978-1-5362-1034-7. This book was typeset in Aged. The illustrations were done in graphite and watercolor.
Candlewick Press, 99 Dover Street, Somerville, Massachusetts 02144. www.candlewick.com.
Printed in Shenzhen, Guangdong, China. 21 22 23 24 25 26 CCP 10 9 8 7 6 5 4 3 2 1